The Blue Stealer

DARREL & SALLY ODGERS

Kane Miller

A DIVISION OF EDC PUBLISHING

JACK RUSSELL: Dog Detective

Book #1 DOG DEN MYSTERY

Book #2 THE PHANTOM MUDDER

Book #3 THE MUGGED PUG

Book #4 THE LYING POSTMAN

Book #5 THE AWFUL PAWFUL

Book #6 THE SAUSAGE SITUATION

Book #7 THE BURIED BISCUITS

Book #8 THE KITNAPPED CREATURE

Book #9 THE BLUE STEALER

First American Edition 2009
by Kane Miller, A Division of EDC Publishing
Tulsa, Oklahoma

First published by Scholastic Australia Pty Limited in 2009
This edition published under license from Scholastic Australia Pty Limited.

Text copyright © Sally and Darrel Odgers, 2009
Interior illustrations © Scholastic Australia, 2009
Cover copyright © Lake Shore Graphics, 2009
Illustrations by Janine Dawson
Jack Russell terrier dog, Frisbee, courtesy of the Cansick family.
Blue Heeler dog, Coco, courtesy of the Diffin family.

All rights reserved.
For information contact:
Kane Miller, A Division of EDC Publishing
P.O. Box 470663
Tulsa, OK 74147-0663
www.kanemiller.com
www.edcpub.com

Library of Congress Control Number: 2009922118
Printed and bound in the United States of America
1 2 3 4 5 6 7 8 9 10
ISBN: 978-1-935279-09-9

Dear Readers,

The story you're about to
read is about me and my friends,
and how we solved the case of the Blue
Stealer. To save time, I'll introduce us all to
you now. If you know us already, you can trot
off to Chapter One.

I am Jack Russell, Dog Detective. I live
with my landlord, Sarge, in Doggeroo. Sarge
detects human-type crimes. I have the
important job of detecting crimes that deal
with dogs. I'm a Jack Russell terrier, so I am
dogged and intelligent. Preacher lives with
us. He is a clever, handsome junior Jack
Russell. His mother is my friend Jill Russell.

Next door to Sarge and me live Auntie
Tidge and Foxie. Auntie Tidge is lovely. She
has biscuits, and fowls. Foxie is not lovely.
He's a fox terrier (more or less). He used to

be a street dog, and a thief, but he's reformed now. Auntie Tidge has even gotten rid of his fleas. Foxie sometimes helps me with my cases.

Uptown Lord Setter (Lord Red for short) lives in Uptown House with Caterina Smith. Lord Red means well, but he isn't very bright.

We have other friends and acquaintances in Doggeroo. These include Polly the dachshund, the Squekes, Ralf Boxer and Shuffle the pug. Then there's Fat Molly, but she's only the cat from the library.

That's all you need to know, so let's get on with Chapter One.

Yours doggedly,

Jack Russell – the detective with a nose for crime.

Changes

"There's a new dog in town," grumbled Foxie. Auntie Tidge had caught him **eyeing** the fowls, so he'd come to visit Preacher and me. "I don't like changes." Foxie put a **paw-sessive** paw on his old boot.

"You didn't mind when Preacher came to live with Sarge and me," I said.

Foxie **muttered**.

I remembered Foxie *had* minded. He'd been jealous of my junior Jack.

"You didn't mind when Sarge and I came to Doggeroo," I said.

Foxie muttered again.

Oops. Foxie had minded that, too. He'd thought I was taking his **terrier-tory**.

"It was a change when you moved in with Auntie Tidge," I said.

Foxie licked his chops. "Auntie Tidge was a good change," he agreed. "The fowls are a bad change." He put his chin on his boot and sulked.

There had been lots of changes since Sarge and I came to Doggeroo. Another one was coming. Sarge and Caterina Smith had decided to get married. When that happened, Preacher and Sarge and I would live with Caterina and Red. Before they got married, they were going to hold a big party for all their friends.

"Where is the new dog, Uncle Foxie?" Preacher asked.

"At the hidden house near the station. Auntie Tidge invited its person to lunch."

"Let's go and visit," said Preacher.

Foxie got up and shook himself. "Might as well." He picked up his boot.

"Leave the boot," I said. Foxie is paw-sessive about his boot. I didn't want squabbles.

Foxie **planted** the boot in the flowerbed near our gate.

We were about to leave our yard (never

mind how) when Caterina Smith arrived in her van.

"Hello, boys!" Caterina staggered a bit as the three of us **greeted** her. She hugged Preacher, and he stuck his nose up under her chin.

Caterina put him down and went to open the back of her van. Lord Red bounced out. "Hello, Foxie. Hello Jack. Hello, Preacher. Are you on a case, Jack? Can I help?"

Foxie scratched himself. "Why not?" he grumbled. "The paw the merrier. Invite Jill Russell and Polly Smote, Shuffle, Ralf Boxer and the Squekes. Invite the whole **Jack-pack**! Let's scare this dog back where it came from."

"What dog?" Red looked confused. "Aren't the Squekes on holiday with Dora Barkins?"

Setters often look confused.
This is because setters find life confusing.
Jack Russells look confused only when there
is something to be confused about.
This is a fact.

"Yes, they are. We're going to visit a dog near the station," I explained.

Red pranced his paws. "Let's go when Caterina Smith takes the box to Auntie Tidge. If she doesn't know I've gone, she won't worry."

Foxie stopped scratching. "What box? Does it have sausages in it?"

Caterina lifted a big cardboard box out of the van. She put it down by the gate. I rose to my hind legs and sniff-sniffed the seam at the top.

"Not a sausage," I reported.

"It's a blue thing with buttons," said Red. "She calls it a dress. She says she wants to look special for the big party."

"Be good, Lordie," said Caterina. "Stay with the others. Don't annoy Auntie Tidge's hens." She carried the box into Foxie's kitchen, and we set off.

Jack's Glossary

Eyeing. *Staring hard at fowls or small furry creatures.*

Paw-sessive. *The way some dogs feel about their homes and belongings.*

Mutter. *A low rumble that is not quite a growl.*

Terrier-tory. *A territory belonging to a terrier.*

Planted. *Something dogs do with their prized paw-sessions to keep them safe.*

Greet. *This is done by rising to the hind legs and clutching a person with the paws while slurping them up the face.*

Jack-pack. *A noble pack of dogs united under a strong leader.*

Blue

As we passed the station, Jill Russell came out. She poked me with her nose, then licked Preacher's ear.

Preacher waggled. "We're going to visit the new dog at Hidden House, Mum. Will you come too?"

Jill Russell wrinkled her nose. "No. His person smells like rubber. He kicks dogs." She kissed Preacher. "I'm off to see Polly Smote and her sprats."

There was a high fence around Hidden House. We sniff-sniffed the wheels of a rusty van parked outside. Foxie did what dogs do to a car. The rest of us did the same, and

tried to aim higher. I was proud of
Preacher's effort, but Red missed the tire
entirely.

I made a **nose map**.

Jack's map:

1. Train smell.

2. Jill Russell.

3. Strange person.

4. Strange dog.

5. Foxie, Red and Preacher.

"The dog is behind the fence," I reported. I applied my **super-sniffer** and sniffed the strange dog's scent. "It's a medium-sized dog," I concluded. "I smell pug … " I **pawsed**.

Why hadn't the new dog challenged us? Was it really there? I sniff-sniffed again. Maybe I'd smelled a dog bed, or a chew toy?

"Hello," I yipped through the gap. "Are you there?"

There was a long pause. Then the dog said, "Who wants to know?"

I introduced us. "I am Jack Russell. My associates are Uptown Lord Setter, Foxie and Preacher."

There was another pause, and then the dog said, "I'm Blue. Where do you live, and what are your best things?"

"I live at Uptown House with Caterina Smith," said Red. "I have a tug toy and a ball and a dog bed and a brush and another ball."

"That's a lot of things for one dog," said Blue.

"I live with Dad and Sarge," said Preacher. "My favorite thing is my chew toy. Dad's got a **squeaker-bone**. Uncle Foxie lives with Auntie Tidge. She has hens. Uncle Foxie has a boot. He planted it at our place."

"It's a **terrier-ably** special boot," growled Foxie.

"A boot!" said Blue. I caught a whiff of pug scent as he moved.

"Are you a pug, Blue?" I asked.

"Whatever gave you that idea?" growled

Blue. "Do I sound like a pug?"

He had a point. Most pugs wheeze a lot.

"I thought I smelled – "

"What?" Blue sounded as if he was hackling.

"Nothing." I was puzzled. What kind of dog smelled like a pug but didn't sound like one? Was he half pug?

"Go away," said Blue. "I can't talk now. Freddy's coming."

The door of the house banged open, and we all backed away and headed home.

"What was that about?" Foxie grumbled. "He was friendly at first, then he wasn't."

A good detective is not ashamed to admit being baffled. I am a good detective.

"I'm baffled," I said.

"Why didn't he want you to think he was a pug?" Red wanted to know.

"Shuffle is a pug," said Preacher. "Did Blue smell like Shuffle, Dad?"

It was only a little mystery, and I didn't spend much time on it. I didn't know then that we'd missed some vital evidence.

As we trotted past the station, the rusty van overtook us. I saw Blue through the window. He was brindled grey, with pricked ears. He was a blue heeler, not a pug.

Jack's Facts

Any kind of dog can be friendly.
Some kinds of dogs are less friendly than others.
Bigger dogs have bigger teeth.
This is a fact.

When we arrived, the rusty van was parked behind Caterina Smith's. Of paws! Auntie Tidge had invited Blue's person for lunch.

We got into Foxie's yard (never mind how), and Foxie disappeared through his **dogdoor**. Preacher followed, wagging.

Red hesitated. "I don't like dogdoors," he reminded me. "They ouch my tail."

Before we settled down to sit on the porch, I sniff-sniffed at the dogdoor. "That's odd," I said. "There's a strange man in the house, but Blue isn't with him. I wonder where he is?"

Just then, a **cackle-cophany** rang out in Foxie's backyard.

Jack's Glossary

Nose map. *Way of storing information collected by the nose.*

Super-sniffer. *Jack's nose in super-tracking mode.*

Pawsed. *Stopped with one paw upraised.*

Squeaker-bone. *Item for exercising teeth. Not to be confused with a toy.*

Terrier-ably. *Very.*

Dogdoor. *A door especially for dogs.*

Cackle-cophany. *A lot of noise made by fowls.*

 Freddy

The front door banged open. Caterina
Smith and Foxie rushed out. They tore
around to the back of the house. Lord Red
sailed off the porch and ran after them.
Preacher zipped out, with Auntie Tidge
puffing behind. The cackle-cophany got
louder, mixed with Foxie's yaps and
scolding from Caterina and Auntie Tidge.

"No, Foxie, no!"

"Lordie! Lordeeeeeeeeeeeeee!"

"Hens! Hens! Mine! Mine!"

"Book-book-book-boo-WARK! Glerk!
Glerk! Boo-gluck-gluck-gluck-BLERK!
WARK!"

Through the din I heard Preacher howl
with excitement. It was his very first howl. I
trotted around to congratulate my junior
Jack, but stopped to stare instead.

Foxie barked and bounced against the
hen pen. Red ran in circles, whirling his tail
and getting in the way. Preacher howled. The
hens had **hen-sterics**. Auntie Tidge and
Caterina tried to catch Foxie and Red.

I sniff-sniffed. I smelled Blue, but I
couldn't see him. He must have ducked

around the front. I returned to the porch in time to see Blue's person, Freddy, close the kitchen door. Blue lay on the porch with his nose on his paws. He lifted his head to look at me with narrow eyes. He was a tough dog. He looked lean and scruffy.

"Hi, Blue, where have you been?" I asked **pawlitely**.

I suspected he'd been flustering the fowls, but I didn't accuse him of the crime. Accusing tough dogs of fowl-flustering is never a good idea. Besides, if I arrested Blue for fowl-flustering, I'd have to arrest Foxie for the same crime.

Blue lifted his lip, and tried to stare me down. "What's it to you where I've been, Jack Russell? This isn't your terrier-tory."

"It's my pal Foxie's terrier-tory," I said. I stared back. *No one* can stare down a Jack.

"Your pal is in trouble," said Blue.

I heard Auntie Tidge scolding Foxie, while Red barked. Preacher stopped howling and scooted back to the porch with his tail low.

"Uncle Foxie is silly," he said. "Let's go, Dad. Sarge is coming home and I want to see him."

"Of paws," I said. "Goodbye, Blue."

Blue turned his head and gave me a kind of sideways stare. It made my hackles itch. But Blue was right. This was Foxie's terrier-tory, not mine. If anyone hackled, it should be Foxie.

Preacher and I crawled under the hedge to greet Sarge.

"Hi, boys. Whatever's going on at Auntie's place?" he asked.

The cackle-cophany was quieting by now.

Auntie Tidge was still scolding Foxie. Sarge leaned on the hedge and called to Caterina. "Caterina! Is everything okay?"

Caterina smiled. "Of course. You know Auntie Tidge is fitting my dress for the party ... *Down*, Lordie! We're doing it here today because she has a visitor for lunch."

"Is that the visitor who's just leaving?" asked Sarge.

I sniff-sniffed under the hedge. Blue and Freddy were heading for their van. They were both lean and tough-looking. They walked in the same way, quickly and quietly.

<u>*Jack's Facts*</u>

People often look like their dogs.
Dogs often look like their people.
Nice people belong to nice dogs.

Nice dogs belong to nice people.
This is a fact.

Sarge went to meet Freddy. Of paws, Preacher and I went too.

Freddy was about to get into the van, but he turned when Caterina called. He pushed Blue into the van, and I ran to sniff-sniff his ankle. Jill Russell was right. He smelled like rubber, and he did kick dogs. I dodged.

"Sarge, this is Freddy – " began Caterina. She broke off as Blue stuck his head out the window and barked three times.

"Quick! Quick! Quick!"

Freddy looked down the street, then smacked Blue on the nose. He hopped into the van. "Gotta go!" he called, and drove off.

"He's in a hurry," said Sarge. "What did

you say his name was?"

"Freddy," said Caterina. "Do you know him?"

"He looks familiar. Maybe I've seen his picture somewhere. Where's Auntie?"

"Shutting Foxie up. He's been bothering the fowls again. By the way, Uncle Smith rang. He's coming to the party, and your brother asked if he can bring – "

Walter Barkley was riding his bike towards us, going very fast. Shuffle sat in a basket at the back. This was unusual, so I yapped and pawed Sarge's leg.

"What's up, Jack?" Sarge bent down to pat me.

I **pointed** with my nose. Sarge turned and looked. "What's the hurry, Walter?" he called. "Is anything wrong?"

Jack's Glossary

Hen-sterics. *Like hysterics. Noisy silliness from hens.*

Pawlite. *Polite, for dogs.*

Pointed. *Clever dogs use their noses to point to things.*

 A Mug of a Pug

Walter Barkley stopped by our gate. He wheezed as loudly as Shuffle. "Oh, Sarge ... I was on my way to the station," he gasped. "We've been burgled!"

Sarge took Walter Barkley into the house. Caterina went to make a **cup of tea**.

Shuffle stayed on the porch with Preacher and Red and me. He lay down with his jaw on his paws and looked **hangdog**.

"What happened, Shuffle?" I asked.

"Walter left me to guard our **territory**. I got **dog-stracted** by a sardine sandwich."

I **interrier-gated** Shuffle. He told me he

had scented the sardine sandwich in the reserve, not long after breakfast. It was **ap-paw-lingly** difficult to track down.

"Why?" I asked.

"It was hidden, in bits," said Shuffle. "It was a game of **seek-the-sandwich**."

"I know that game, Jack!" put in Red. "Sarge plays it with me when he has lunch with Caterina Smith. Maybe Sarge left the sardine sandwich as a present for Shuffle."

"Of paws not!" I told Red. "Sarge was at work, not playing seek-the-sandwich."

Preacher watched closely, but he didn't **interr-pup-t**. I was proud of him.

"Where was Walter Barkley while you played seek-the-sandwich?" I asked.

Shuffle snuffled. "He took the train to Jeandabah Hennery to buy laying pellets for our hen. He left me on guard."

"And you were dog-stracted."

"I failed in my duty to Walter Barkley," said Shuffle. "While I played seek-the-sandwich, someone stole Walter Barkley's television set and other things." He looked up at me with gloomy eyes. "I am a mug of a pug."

Preacher licked Shuffle's ear. "Dad will detect the criminal."

"Of paws!" said Red. "Jack Russell's the name, detection's the game ... right, Jack?"

"I am a *dog* detective," I reminded them. "This is a human matter, with a human villain and a human victim."

"There's a dog victim too," said Preacher. "Shuffle feels bad. It's the criminal's fault."

I wanted to wash my paws of this crime, but Preacher had put *his* paw on the problem. Shuffle was in trouble. It *was* a case for the dog detective.

"Will you take the case, Jack?" asked Red.

I poked my nose in my basket and fetched my squeaker-bone from under the blanket Auntie Tidge knitted. I had a good chew. Exercising my jaws helps me think.

Shuffle sighed, and snuffled.

Jack's Facts

Pugs never look pawfully happy.
A sad and sorry pug is a sad and sorry sight.
This is a fact.

"I'll take the case." I put my paw on my squeaker-bone and sat up. "Shuffle, you are a witness. Your evidence is vital."

"I didn't see anything," said Shuffle.

"Maybe you *smelled* something?"

"Only the sardine sandwich," gloomed Shuffle. "I don't have a super-sniffer like a terrier, but even I can smell a sardine – "

"Exactly!" I exclaimed. "Now I see what happened!"

I didn't see it all, but I did see some of it.

Jack's Glossary

Cup of tea. *Something soothing for humans.*

Hangdog. *Miserable, with tail hanging low.*

Territory. *The terrier-tory owned by a dog who is not a terrier.*

Dog-stracted. *Distracted by a dog, or attempt to distract a dog.*

Interrier-gated. *Official questioning, done by a terrier.*

Ap-paw-lingly. *Like appallingly or badly, but for dogs.*

Seek-the-sandwich. *A game that dogs should play only with trusted humans.*

Interr-pup-t. *Interrupt, done by a junior dog.*

Booty

Red and Preacher looked hopeful. Even
Shuffle lifted his jaw from his paws.

"Describe how the sandwich was
hidden," I instructed.

"There was a piece in a hollow log. I
used my paw to get that. Another piece
was in a rabbit hole. I had to dig for that."

I didn't want to **lead the witness**, but
I had to **keep him on track**. "Was the
first piece of sandwich close to your
guard post?"

Shuffle sat up straight. "It was just
past the fence. I tracked that down, and

the next one was a bit farther on. Our hen came with me. She ate the crumbs."

"You see what this means?" I looked at Red and Preacher.

"Someone wanted Shuffle to follow a trail," said Preacher.

"Good," I said. "If I'm right, the sardine sandwich is at the very heart of the matter."

"I thought you put sardines in your tummy," said Red.

I **ig-gnawed** that.

"The sandwich had three roles in the crime," I said. "One. Sardines have a strong scent. Therefore, Shuffle whiffed them from a distance. This allowed the criminal to lure the faithful guard from his post without getting close.

"Two. Dogs like sardines. Therefore, Shuffle tracked all the pieces. This gave the criminal time for crime while Shuffle was dog-stracted.

"Three. The sardines masked any other scent at the crime scene."

I thought of another role the sardines might play. "Shuffle, do you feel all right?"

"I feel like a mug of a pug," gloomed Shuffle.

Preacher jumped up and poked Shuffle with his nose. "Dad thinks the sandwich was **doggled** with sleepy stuff. Are you sleepy? Do you have a bellyache? Is your nose hot?"

"No!" said Shuffle.

"That tells us something else about the criminal," I said. "The criminal wanted to lure Shuffle from his post, but not to hurt him."

I felt proud of my deductions, but what came next? Knowing the criminal knew how to lure honest dogs didn't tell me who it was. We were about to visit the scene of the crime to sniff for evidence (and to eat leftover lures), when our people came out.

"Come to the station, Walter, to make a report," Sarge said. "Shuffle can stay here with the other dogs."

"I'm going to Auntie for my dress fitting," Caterina told Sarge. "I'll see you later."

I had just **pawposed** a trip to the crime scene when Foxie crawled under our hedge. He looked as hangdog as Shuffle.

"I have been **unjustly accused** of fowl-flustering. I need my boot," he said.

"What makes you think we have it?" Red asked.

Foxie sat down and scratched his elbows. "I left it here, remember? I planted it before we went to visit Blue."

"We have a case," I said. "There's been a crime at Shuffle's territory. We're going to sniff for evidence."

Foxie scratched his ear. "I'll stay and chew my boot."

Red, Preacher, Shuffle and I left our yard (never mind how). We were halfway to the reserve when we heard a howl and a patter of paws. Foxie raced up behind us.

"I thought you were going to chew your boot," said Red.

"I can't!" snarled Foxie. "Someone's stolen it! This is *your* fault, Jack Russell."

I stared at my pal. He stared back. His

hackles were up.

"Don't be silly," I said briskly. "Why would I steal your boot? You're my pal."

"I didn't say you stole it," howled Foxie. "But it's your fault it was stolen. You made me leave it behind this morning."

Of paws, we went back to our yard, and sniff-sniffed where Foxie had planted the boot. My super-sniffer detected where the boot had been, but not where it was now. Too many tracks led through our yard, crossing and re-crossing.

I turned to my pals. "Nose map this yard," I ordered. "Ig-gnaw scents like birds and moths. Just map people and dogs."

We got to work. Even Shuffle helped, although pugs' **sniffers** are not well-placed for nose mapping. When we finished, we made a Jack-pack map.

Our Jack-pack map:

1. My tracks.

2. Preacher's tracks.

3. Foxie's tracks.

4. Red's tracks.

5. Shuffle's tracks.

6. Blue's tracks.

7. Sarge's tracks.

8. Caterina's tracks.

9. Walter Barkley's tracks.

"We can **eliminate** me from the list of suspects," I said. "Preacher and Red can be eliminated too."

"Why?" snarled Foxie. "You have motives. It's a terrier-ably special boot. Any dog would want it."

"We were with you," I reminded him. "You planted the boot and we went to visit Blue. That puts Blue in the clear too. He couldn't steal your boot while he was talking to us."

"Shuffle stole it, then!" snapped Foxie.

"I didn't!" said Shuffle. "After I finished playing seek-the-sandwich I waited for Walter Barkley to come home. Maybe your humans did it."

"They wouldn't," I said. "If Sarge found Foxie's boot in our yard, he would drop it over the hedge. Besides, Sarge came home *after* we did. Caterina Smith, Walter Barkley and Shuffle came into our yard *after* Sarge came home. We would have seen if they took the boot."

It was a mystery. At some point after Preacher, Red, Foxie and I went to visit Blue, Foxie's old boot had become someone's **booty**.

Jack's Glossary

Lead the witness. *Give a witness ideas.*

Keep him on track. *Make a witness stick to the point.*

Ig-gnawed. *Ignored, but done by dogs.*

Doggled. *Filled with sleeping medicine to quieten a dog.*

Pawpose. *Like propose, but for dogs.*

Unjustly accused. *Accused of doing something someone else did.*

Sniffer. *A dog's nose in tracking mode. Only Jack Russell terriers have super-sniffers.*

Eliminate. *Leave out, take away.*

Booty. *Anything carried off by a criminal.*

Blue Stealer?

"I want my boot," growled Foxie. "Jack, detect the criminal."

"Is it you, Uncle Foxie?" asked Preacher.

I wondered that myself. Foxie used to be a pawfully clever **canine criminal**.

"Foxie?" I asked. "You once stole my squeaker bone, and Caterina's sausages."

Foxie's hackles popped up, and he glared. "You'd taken my terrier-tory, and those sausages were mine by right!" Then he calmed down. "Not guilty, Jack. Most of the dogs in Doggeroo had motives."

"Maybe, but they had no means or **op-paw-tunity**. Ralf Boxer is too small to carry off this booty. Polly Smote has sprats to look after. Jill Russell went to visit Polly. We can check her **alibi**, but I don't believe Jill Russell stole the boot. Jill wasn't on our Jack-pack map."

"Your alibi is shaky," growled Foxie. "When we came back from meeting Blue, you stayed outside. You could have taken it then."

I hadn't, but Foxie was right. I could have done it then. I listed the order of events. "We came back from Blue's. You and Preacher went through the dogdoor. Red and I stayed on the porch. The cackle-cophany started. You and Caterina Smith rushed out. Red followed you. Preacher came out next, with

Auntie Tidge. When Preacher howled, I followed. Freddy stayed in the kitchen. When I got back, Blue was on the porch, but he must have only just got there."

Foxie bristled. "I think Blue is a blue stealer!"

I remembered my earlier suspicions. "I think Blue may have set off the cackle-cophany," I said. "You kept it going,

Foxie, but you ran out *after* it started."

"Rrrrright," growled Foxie. "While we were all dog-stracted by the cackle-cophany, that blue stealer stole my boot!"

"But did he have time? Sarge came home, remember?"

"Blue heelers are speedy," said Red. "Blue heelers are slick, quick and sly. They get wicked if they have too much time on their paws. They turn into blue stealers."

We all stared at Red. "How do you know that?" I asked.

"There's a blue heeler called Barley at Uncle Smith's farm near Cowfork," said Red. "She told me she used to be a bad, bad dog, but now she's reformed. Blue's a blue heeler too. You can tell by his **brindles**."

Wishing Red had mentioned that *before*, I chewed the idea in my mind. I checked our

Jack-pack map. Everyone had an alibi except
for the blue stealer.

<u>Jack's Facts</u>

If most dogs have alibis and one dog doesn't,
that dog is probably a canine criminal.
This is a fact.

"His scent was on our map," I reminded
my pals. "Maybe he committed the crime in
two stages. He and Freddy got to Auntie
Tidge's *before* we got home. He might have
taken the booty then and hidden it near the
hen pen. After we got home, he moved it.
That made the hens have hen-sterics."

"Interrier-gate the hens," suggested
Preacher.

"**Impawsible**," I reminded him. "Dogs

know only **dogspeak**. Hens know only **henspeak**."

"I know **catspeak**," objected Preacher. "Fat Molly teaches me buzzing."

I hackled at Foxie, and he didn't comment on this.

"Fat Molly stole my boot," he said instead. "I'll bite her tail until she confesses."

"Uncle Foxie!" yelped Preacher. "Molly's my *pal*! You don't bite your pal's pal's tail!"

"I do if my pal's pal steals my boot," said Foxie.

Things were getting out of paw. I **Jack-yapped** for attention. "Fat Molly is a cranky, crabby, sneaky, slippery *cat*," I said. "But she did not take the booty. It is too heavy for a cat of Molly's size. I am convinced that the blue stealer took the booty. He is a canine criminal."

"Arrest him," suggested Red.

"That won't be easy," I admitted. "Besides, the blue stealer is not the only criminal in Doggeroo. It was not the blue stealer who lured Shuffle from his post and stole Walter Barkley's treasures." I made a decision. "We'll sniff-sniff for evidence at the crime scene. On the way back, we'll in-terrier-gate the blue stealer and recover the booty."

Jack's Glossary

Canine criminal. *A bad dog.*

Op-paw-tunity. *Opportunity, for dogs.*

Alibi. *The thing a dog was doing that made it impawsible for him to be somewhere else.*

Brindles. *Squiggle patterns on the coat. Jack Russell terriers do not have these.*

Impawsible. *Impossible, for dogs.*

Dogspeak. *The private language of dogs.*

Henspeak. *The way hens talk.*

Catspeak. *The way cats talk.*

Jack-yap. *A loud, piercing yap made by a Jack Russell terrier.*

Crime Scene

When we arrived at the crime scene, Sarge and Walter Barkley were there.

Normally, I would have greeted Sarge, but today we were both busy. He had one case. I had two. I told Red, Foxie and Preacher to wait at Shuffle's guard post while I used my super-sniffer.

"And don't eye Walter's hen!" I ordered Foxie.

Shuffle came with me to point the way.

Jack's Facts

Most dogs have noses at the end of their faces.

Pugs keep their noses in a different place.
Therefore, it isn't easy for a pug to point
to things.
This is a fact.

I found the site of the first lure.
Shuffle and the hen had eaten every
crumb, but the smell of sardine
sandwiches lingered.

By the time I'd followed up all the
lures, Sarge was leaving.

"I'm sorry, Walter. It looks like a
professional job. Our crook probably
wore gloves. Did anyone know you were
going to be away?"

"Jack and Jill Johnson at the station
knew, but they're not thieves."

"Get your locks changed," advised
Sarge. "Maybe the items will turn up. I'll

send a description to Inspector Kipper in the city. Television, antique clock, gold pocket watch ... anything else?"

"No," said Walter. "Apart from poor old Shuffle's pug cloth."

Sarge laughed. "I don't think that was part of the booty, Walter." He spotted us. "Looks like the dogs followed us. I'll take ours back."

"Come, Shuffle," said Walter. "We'll look for your pug cloth."

We were on our way home when I thought of something. "What's a pug cloth?"

"It's cloth for cleaning pug wrinkles," said Red. "Pugs' people take them to shows."

"I see ... " I said. "I *see!*" I jumped up and dabbed my nose against Sarge's hand. He had given me another clue. I dabbed Red as well. "Red, you're a pawfully clever dog sometimes."

Preacher, Foxie and Red all stared at me, then Red pranced his paws.

"You think so, Jack? That's great ... but what did I do that was clever?"

"You gave me a piece of the puzzle." We were close to the station now, level with Blue's gate. "You remember I said Blue smelled like a pug?"

"He got cross," said Preacher.

"Now I know why. Foxie's boot isn't the first bit of booty the blue stealer stole. He'd taken Shuffle's pug cloth first! That's what we smelled under his gate. We didn't detect him at the crime scene because of the sardines."

"You had better interrier-gate him," said Red.

"And get my boot back!" snarled Foxie.

I wasn't looking forward to this interrier-gation, but I agreed with my pals. We stopped by the blue stealer's gate.

Sarge stopped, too. "Jack?" Then he shrugged. "I have to get to work. You go home." He went on past the station.

I applied my super-sniffer to the gap underneath. I sniff-sniffed. Yes, I smelled pug – that must be Shuffle's pug cloth. Foxie stuck his sniffer under the gap as well.

"My boot!" he yapped. He began to
scratch at the gate, sniffing and scrabbling.
"My boot! Gimme my boot!"

With the din Foxie made, I expected the
blue stealer to react. Nothing happened.

I nipped Foxie's ear. "Stop in the name of
the paw!"

Foxie spun round. "I'll get you for that,
Jack Russell! It's my property!"

"The blue stealer is not there," I said.
"Nor is Freddy."

Strong Warning

It was time to close one of my cases. The blue stealer was out, so I couldn't arrest him. But we *could* reclaim Foxie's boot and Shuffle's pug cloth.

"He's probably stealing something else," said Foxie.

"We'll leave a strong warning," I decided. "When he knows we know he's a blue stealer, he'll give up."

We entered the blue stealer's territory. Jacks jump over. Jacks burrow under. Jacks crawl through. **Paw-tunately**, fox terriers are also **digging dogs**, so Foxie followed me. We

left Red on guard.

Foxie pounced on his boot. It was lying just inside the gate. A big soft cloth was tucked inside it. It smelled of pug and Walter Barkley. Next to it was a plastic chop. I recognized that, too. It smelled of the Squekes. The blue stealer *had* been busy.

Foxie rolled on his boot, kicking and growling with joy.

We had recovered the booty. Now for the strong warning.

There are lots of ways to give warnings. Growling, staring and stalking all work. Ig-gnawing a dog sometimes works. Of course, the dog has to be there.

The blue stealer was not there, so we **pawtrolled** the **pawrimeter** of his territory. We stopped every few steps to do what dogs do to mark territory.

"Will weeing on the blue stealer's fence stop him stealing, Dad?" asked Preacher.

"He invaded other territories," I explained. "First we show him we can invade his. Then we take away his booty. Next, we alert the Jack-pack. Every dog in Doggeroo must keep its treasures safe from the blue stealer."

"We should take *his* treasures," growled Foxie.

"What treasures?" Preacher wanted to know.

My junior Jack had a point. The only treasures we detected belonged to other dogs. We pawtrolled again. No blanket. No dog bed. No balls. No tug toys. No squeakers. We didn't find a bowl, just scraps. Foxie sniffed and turned up his nose.

We sniff-sniffed around the shed. There was a faint whiff of pug, Walter Barkley, the Squekes and Dora Barkins. We also detected rubber, oil and polish. I sneezed.

We were still busy when Red barked. "Jack! Caterina is calling me."

"Time to go," I said. If Red left, we would have no guard. Besides, we had delivered our strong warning.

We gathered up the booty and left the blue stealer's territory just in time. Caterina had caught up with Red, and Freddy's rusty van was headed our way. Preacher, Foxie and I scooted towards the station.

Jill Russell was waiting. "You were in that dog's territory," she said. "Did you ask

pawmission? You've got the Squekes' chop. Did they say you could borrow it?"

Foxie dropped his boot, and put his paw on it. "We reclaimed some booty. The blue stealer didn't ask pawmission before he invaded our terrier-tory."

"Dad solved the case," said Preacher proudly.

"We solved *one* case," I corrected. "We have booty belonging to Foxie, Shuffle and the Squekes. We warned a criminal. *But* we don't know who left the sardine sandwiches."

"Sardines?" Jill Russell looked interested. "Rubber-smelly Freddy had sardines. He kicked me when I **asked** for some."

Of paws, I kissed Jill Russell. She had given me another good piece of the puzzle.

"The cases are connected," I said. "The blue stealer steals dogs' treasures. His person steals from people. They work as a team." I reminded Foxie and Preacher how Blue barked a warning as Walter Barkley and Shuffle appeared. "Freddy left in a hurry," I said. "He thought Shuffle would point to him."

We had solved both cases, but what now? Jack Russell terriers are brave, intelligent dogs. But we are not big enough to arrest human criminals.

"We must show Sarge the evidence," I decided. "That will get a result."

We hurried home, but Sarge wasn't there. As we entered our dogdoor, the **terrier-phone** rang. The answering machine clicked.

"Sarge?" said Caterina's voice. "I called the station, but you weren't back. We've been burgled. My rings are gone. So are Grandma's silver set and the engagement presents."

Caterina's voice kept going, but we heard Red bark behind her. "Jack! Jack! My tug toy is gone. I suspect the blue stealer!"

Since Sarge wasn't there, we ran to Auntie Tidge. She was on the terrier-phone.

"It's dreadful, dear!" Auntie Tidge said. "Dora Barkins is away, so I went to feed her fowls. Someone has been in her house. I don't know *what* ... Yes, I left a message with the young constable. He said Sarge – wait! I hear him now."

So did we. I shot out the dogdoor and raced to meet him.

Jack's Glossary

Paw-tunately. *Fortunately.*

Digging dog. *Different dogs are good at different things. Terriers dig. Setters run.*

Pawtrolled. *Patrolled, for dogs.*

Pawrimeter. *The outside of a dog's terrier-tory.*

Pawmission. *Permission, given by a dog.*

Ask. *Staring, whining and pawing at people's legs. Pawlite dogs don't ask too often.*

Terrier-phones. *Things that ring.*

Jack-Pack

Sarge was in a terrier-able rush. "Not *now*, Jack!" he said. "Stay!"

Auntie Tidge puffed up. "Dear, someone broke in to Dora's house! And poor Caterina has been burgled. You must – "

"Sorry, Auntie," said Sarge. "Inspector Kipper called. He has a lead for us, so I'm taking the train. Can you let Caterina know? And mind Jack and Preacher?"

"Yes, but *dear* – "

"Got to go!" Sarge raced out our gate and off towards the station.

I *had* to stop him. Inspector Kipper is clever, but the thief was here in Doggeroo! I dove after Sarge. My junior Jack and Foxie were behind me. Preacher howled and Foxie yapped. Together, they summoned the Jack-pack.

The streets of Doggeroo rang as our friends passed the message to form the pack.

I had just one mission.

Stop Sarge!

As we reached the station, a dozen dogs swept past to Hidden House. They had no idea what had happened. They just obeyed my orders.

"Stop Sarge! Don't let anyone leave that yard!"

I **Jack-attacked** Sarge's trouser leg and made him stop. Meanwhile, the Jack-pack scrabbled and sniffed and barked and yapped outside the blue stealer's territory. This time, I knew the territory was occupied.

"All *right*, Jack!" yelled Sarge.

Jill Russell's people rushed out. "Jill! Jill! What ... ?"

Other people arrived, looking for their dogs, or yelling about the noise. Lord Red bounded down the road, with Caterina running after him.

Sarge held up his hands. "Calm down! I don't know what's going on, but the dogs seem to think there's something wrong. Does anyone know who might be in there? I thought this place was empty."

"No, that new chap moved in a few days ago," said Jack Johnson. "Freddy something."

"Freddy Wysell," said Tina Boxer. "He picked up his mail from my shop."

"Freddy Wysell ... Hmm, that name seems familiar." Sarge banged on the gate. "Freddy? Are you in there? Are you in trouble?"

He was still banging when an engine roared inside the yard. Then came a crunch and the high gates shook. We all jumped aside as they smashed open, and the van shot out through the mashed-up wood. It swerved hard around the crowd, and the back door banged open.

The Jack-pack scattered as a heap of shiny spoons and one blue stealer landed on the road.

Blue yelped and snarled. The van roared away, and Sarge dashed to call for backup.

Caterina stared. "Those are our spoons!" she said.

Jack's Glossary

Jack-attack. *Growling and biting and worrying at trouser legs. Very loud. Quite harmless.*

What Happened Afterwards

That was almost the end of the case of the blue stealer, but lots of things happened afterwards. Some of them were to do with the case. Some of them weren't.

First, I arrested Blue. Caterina helped me. So did Foxie and Preacher and Red. He didn't come quietly, so we handed him over to Ranger Jack.

Meanwhile, Sarge arrested Freddy, and that was the last we saw of him in Doggeroo. It turned out that Freddy "Hydraulic Fingers" Wysell was a **wanted criminal**. Inspector Kipper explained that when he came to

Doggeroo for the big party.

"Wysell used to move from town to town. He'd rent a house near a station or bus depot. When he saw people go out, he'd break into their houses. He would get as much loot as he could as fast as he could. Then he'd pack up his van and move on somewhere else to sell it. He had that dog trained to help steal. If his dog got into a property without being detected, Fingers Wysell would follow."

Auntie Tidge clicked her tongue. "Just think! He burgled Walter's place, then came to lunch with us. Then he went on to burgle Uptown House while Caterina was with me."

"The scheme worked every time," said Inspector Kipper. "But something must have gone wrong when he tried it in Doggeroo."

"It was the dogs," said Sarge. "Some of them must have tracked their owners' possessions to where Freddy had stored them."

<u>Jack's Facts</u>

Sarge is a clever person.
Even clever people sometimes get hold of **the wrong end of the stick.**
This is a fact.

Inspector Kipper rubbed my ears. "Fingers Wysell will be in prison for quite a while. I suppose it's the **end of the road** for *his* dog. I can't imagine anyone wanting it for a pet."

I felt a bit hangdog about that. Blue was not a nice dog, but that was because Freddy Wysell was not a nice person. Dogs want to trust their owners. If the owners are bad, it can make a dog go bad too.

But it wasn't the end for Blue. Caterina's

Uncle Smith came to Doggeroo that afternoon. When he heard the news, he offered Blue a new home on his farm.

"Blue heelers are working dogs," he said. "Blue has been taught to steal. If he comes to live with me and Barley, we can train him to do other things. With a bit of good food and proper attention, he'll be fine. He'll be a happier dog, and that means he'll be a nicer dog."

So, I'm pleased to report that the blue stealer has a new home. I'm also pleased to report that it isn't in Doggeroo. This brought the case of the blue stealer to a **successful conclusion**.

The day after that, Foxie and his boot disappeared.

Preacher, Red and I tracked them down to the river, where Polly Smote lives.

Mother dogs don't like visitors when their sprats are tiny. But now Polly's sprats were big enough to waggle their tails and yip. They were rolling around, growling and playing. Foxie was watching from a safe distance, keeping his paw on his boot.

"What are you doing here, Foxie?" asked Red. "Have you run away?"

"Of paws not," grumbled Foxie. "Can't a dog come and visit another dog? You three might be my pals, but you're not my *only* pals."

Preacher poked his nose into the basket of sprats. "Look, Dad! This fuzzy one is just

like Trump and Jackie and Wednesday!"

I reminded him that his sisters were grown up now, like him.

Preacher sniff-sniffed a girl sprat. "Look at that spotty one, Dad! She's just like Uncle Foxie."

"Foxie is a fox terrier," I said. "These are dachshund sprats."

"She still looks like Uncle Foxie. Look, she's scratching her elbows, and she's got an old shoe to play with."

Spotty Sprat caught my eye. She put her paw on the old shoe. "Mine! Mine! Mine!" she yipped.

I remembered dogs can be made up of more than one breed ...

The day after *that,* Sarge and Caterina held their big party at Uptown House. This was to let all their friends get to know one another now that they had decided to get married. I tried to nose map everyone there, but in the end I gave up. There were people and dogs everywhere.

Auntie Tidge set Foxie on **clean up duty**. Of paws, it was my duty to help my pal. We were dealing with scraps of sausage roll when Preacher came to find me. He was waggling his tail.

"Dad, I saw a special dog. She came with a man who smells like Sarge."

"Of course you saw a dog," said Foxie. He spluttered crumbs, and belched. "There are always dogs, coming and going. There are new dogs and old dogs and sprat dogs and dogs that interr-pup-t. And sometimes there's a dog who wants to steal another dog's treasure." Foxie checked his old boot.

Since he'd got it back, he carried it everywhere.

"This is a *special* dog, Dad," pawsisted Preacher. "She's a senior Jack Russell. She said I had to find you and tell you to come and see her *right away*. That is an order!"

Jacks do not take orders from other dogs.
Jacks give orders to other dogs.
The only dog that can give an order to a Jack
is a special senior Jack.
This is a fact.

I made a new nose map to check the facts, putting the special dog right in the middle. Preacher was pawfectly correct.

My mother, Ace, was a very special dog. Of paws I went to see her *right away*.

Jack's map:

Jack's Glossary

Wanted criminals. *People who do bad things until they're stopped.*

Getting the wrong end of the stick. *Misunderstanding something that is pawfectly clear to dogs.*

End of the road. *Not a good place for a dog to find itself.*

Successful conclusion. *An ending where everything turns out properly. The human criminal is arrested. The canine criminal gets a new chance. The detective is proud of his work. There is plenty to eat, and everyone has a big party.*

Clean up duty. *Cleaning up food that has fallen to the ground.*

JACK RUSSELL: Dog Detective

Read all of Jack's adventures!

Jack Russell:
the detective with
a nose for crime.